TAHOSA
TREASURE

TAHOSA TREASURE

A Talon Family Story

HANNAH McKAY & JEFF ROTH

TATE PUBLISHING
AND ENTERPRISES, LLC

Published by Tate Publishing & Enterprises, LLC
127 E. Trade Center Terrace | Mustang, Oklahoma 73064 USA
1.888.361.9473 | www.tatepublishing.com

Tate Publishing is committed to excellence in the publishing industry. The company reflects the philosophy established by the founders, based on Psalm 68:11,
"The Lord gave the word and great was the company of those who published it."

Book design copyright © 2012 by Tate Publishing, LLC. All rights reserved.
Cover design by Rtor Maghuyop
Interior design by Caypeeline Casas

Published in the United States of America

ISBN: 978-1-62295-115-4
1. Fiction / Action & Adventure
2. Fiction / Suspense
12.09.27

CHAPTER 1

JULY 1968

A slight breeze stirred the tops of the tall Ponderosa pines that afternoon in Tahosa Valley. The animals rested in their holes and dens to escape the heat of the day. A group of bull elk were bedded down in an aspen grove.

"Come on, Dazzle! Come on!" urged the boy, Jeb Talon, as he clung to the mane of his Belgium workhorse.

He was racing his oldest brother, Jack, who was behind him on Red, a roan gelding. The husky workhorse had the lean gelding outdistanced by at least two lengths; Dazzle loved to run, and Red would have preferred resting in the shade.

The four of them crashed through the underbrush, straight into the aspen grove. The bulls startled up into wild flight, causing Dazzle to rear and then buck. Jeb held tightly to Dazzle's mane, but it was no use; he flew through the air, hitting a dead tree and knocking it down in the process.

Jeb landed hard on his back with a thud. His glasses, held together with cloth tape after a previous break, landed several feet away still intact. Dazzle immediately quit bucking and tore off a short distance up the valley, stopping to graze as though nothing had happened.

Realizing Jeb was fine, Jack began to laugh. To save face, Jeb tried to act like he was seriously hurt, rolling on the ground and moaning. But soon he was laughing as he pictured how funny he must have looked flying through the air.

"What's going on?" Ben, their middle brother, asked as he rode up to the scene on his horse, Sadie. Jack began to explain as he got down from his horse to help Jeb, but his words trailed off as he walked to the base of the dead aspen and grabbed a steel rod partially imbedded in the ground. It took a minute to free it.

"Hey, guys, can you help me find my glasses?" Jeb asked as he stood and brushed himself off.

"They're just behind your right heel," Ben replied. Jeb grabbed his glasses, put them on, and then stopped as he saw Jack with the steel rod in his hands.

"What's that?" he asked with a puzzled look on his face.

"I don't know," Jack said. "Looks like an old rifle barrel. What do you make of it, Ben?" Jack handed it to his brother.

Ben turned it over in his hands, thinking, trying to remember where he had seen it before. He had a vague recollection but could not place it. "I think you're right," Ben said. "Looks like an old rifle barrel. Why don't we take it to Grandpa's birthday party? He'll know what type of gun it belonged to."

"I saw a small creek a little ways back," Jack said, taking the barrel and Red's lead line. "I'll clean it up, and then we can head back."

"I'll go catch Dazzle," Jeb said, starting toward the Belgium who was happily munching green grass. Jack was able to clean up the outside of the barrel in the creek and found a willow branch skinny enough to push out the dirt and debris that had been jammed inside. They met at the creek and headed toward home, riding single file through the woods.

The three Talon brothers were a familiar trio in the Tahosa Valley. Jack had dark brown hair and was tougher than most twelve year olds. He could think fast on his feet, always had an answer, and was usually right. He was more than just the leader by default—he sought the position and held it.

Ben was eleven, tall for his age, quiet, and followed his older brother with a measured step and a watchful eye. He was a good balance to Jack's stronger personality, willing to follow, and giving input only when asked. He trusted Jack's decision-making skills, and Jack, in turn, respected Ben's advice.

The last part of the trio was nine-year-old Jeb. Even though he was the youngest, he was the most daring and impulsive of the three with his charge-ahead mentality. His glasses held together at the bridge with cloth tape were evidence of this. His blue eyes shone with a spark of curiosity and adventure. He had neither the mature decision-making skills of Jack nor the thoughtful cautiousness of Ben, but he had guts enough for both.

It was the tenth of July and their grandpa, Otto Talon's, birthday. The Talon family members had come to help celebrate. It was a big affair since this was Grandpa Otto's sixtieth birthday.

To the Talon family, birthdays were times to gather and share stories. Heritage was very important to them. As a special birthday gift, Aunt Rita, Grandpa Otto's daughter who had not been able to come, sent a photo album with pictures and entries written in her careful hand. It was the history of the Talon Family in Tahosa Valley.

After "Happy Birthday" had been sung and the cake had been cut and everyone sat around with full stomachs, Grandpa Otto began to read from the book. A hush fell over everybody. Jeb, Jack, and Ben listened attentively and even the youngest cousins were quiet.

The Talon Family has lived in Tahosa Valley for three generations. Great-Grandpa Chris Talon came from Illinois as one of the original homesteaders in the late 1800s. During the early 1920s, Great-Grandpa Chris Talon was able to buy three additional half section homesteads. His son, Otto, was born in 1908 in the original cabin on Tahosa Creek.

"That's you, Grandpa! That's you!" a young grandchild broke in excitedly.

Grandpa Otto smiled and nodded. "So it is," he said and continued to read.

Otto grew up working the ranch and in 1919 apprenticed as a machinist for Springfield Armory back east. He started out making the model 1903 Springfield rifle. Otto Talon came from a long line of gunsmiths from the Alps of Southern Germany.

In 1929, Otto returned home to Tahosa Valley when he inherited the homestead after Great-Grandpa Chris Talon passed away. Great-Grandmother Ida Talon survived Great-Grandpa several more years, and then she too passed away and was buried beside Great-Grandpa near Lost

Cabin. In the summer of 1930, Otto married a fine woman named Greta.

Here Grandpa Otto reached out and took his wife's hand. He squeezed it, and she laid her hand on top of his and smiled. Anyone could tell that they were still as happy as when they had married over thirty-eight years before.

Their son, Royal, was born in 1931 and their daughter, Rita, four years later. Royal and Rita grew up working the ranch in Tahosa Valley. Royal married his college sweetheart, Sara, the year he graduated. They took on the responsibilities of the ranch and started their family. Rita married and moved out of the Valley, but it still remained in her heart.

Part of the land was sold to those who might want a summer place in the mountains and part of the land was used to build a Christian youth camp. For three months during the summer, churches would band together and send a different age group every week to spend time in the mountains and learn more about creation and its Creator. The arduous life of ranching was made worthwhile by the joy of seeing many campers receive Christ each summer.

Otto and Greta still live in the Valley and enjoy their children and grandchildren, family and friends. The Tahosa Valley is a part of all of them and always will be.

After the story had been told, the conversation turned to other subjects, and Jack brought out the barrel they had found and handed it to his grandpa.

"We found this today, Grandpa, in the upper pasture. Is it a rifle barrel?"

Grandpa looked at the outside and inside and studied both ends of the barrel. Finally he said, "I don't believe it's a rifle barrel in the strictest sense but a *musket* barrel." He held it up. "See…the inside is smooth. A musket had a smooth bore and, later when little ridges or rifling were added to make the aim of the bullet more accurate, guns started to be called *rifles*." He hefted it in his hand. "So this was once part of a musket. The rest of the gun has rotted away. I'll bet if you go back and look very closely you'll find the lock or firing mechanism."

Ben and Jeb had come to stand by them now, as well as their father, Royal. "When did they stop using muskets, Dad?" Royal asked. "Wasn't it some time around the Civil War?"

"Around about that time, yes," Grandpa replied. A sort of half-smile flitted across his face, and he seemed to be remembering something. "Just like Rita's book said, the Talon's come from a long line of gunsmiths. Family folklore has it that our ancestors emigrated from Germany in the late 1600s. Our surname was originally 'Traugott.' In those days, gunsmiths put a symbol on the barrel to show pride in their workmanship, and we used a symbol of a talon. Over time, we began to be known as the 'Talons,' and we eventually changed our surname to simplify things." Grandpa Otto looked down and studied the barrel again. "This barrel is pock-marked and rusted, but I don't see a symbol on it anywhere."

"How do you think the barrel got by the tree?" Jeb asked, his eyes alight with boyhood curiosity.

"Who knows?" said Grandpa. "Your guess is as good as mine. Tahosa Valley was a pretty tough place to live, up until I was a youngster." He laid a hand on his youngest grandson's shoulder. "When I was younger than you, Jeb, I remember an old timer who lived up near House Rock. He used to stop by around dinnertime. Mother didn't like him much because he always smelled, but Father and I loved his old stories of the Valley. One day we realized we hadn't seen him in awhile, and Father and I went up to his bachelor cabin to make sure he wasn't sick or hurt. We couldn't find him and never figured out what happened to him."

Grandpa Otto handed the gun barrel back to Jack, settled in his chair, and folded his hands. His face still had the look of remembering as he continued. "There are also many stories of Spaniards, Indians, and mountain men fighting and hunting in this valley. I do remember one interesting story... Back in the early forties when they were making Highway 7, I think, near Aspen Lodge, they uncovered a mass grave with several remains in it. I remember that the archeologist they brought in believed they were once Spanish soldiers based on some of the artifacts they found. I always wondered what had happened to those soldiers. They said the arrowhead and hatchet marks on the skulls and other bones showed that they were probably killed by Indians. You've got to wonder what kind of battle took place to kill so many men at one time."

CHAPTER 2

LATE SUMMER 1803

Standing Elk had a decision to make. The day was crisp. The late summer sky was cloudless. He had found a vantage point sitting among some boulders near the top of present day Estes Cone at eleven thousand feet. This spot gave him a commanding view of both Tahosa Valley to the south and large parks and meadows to the north in what would one day be called Estes Valley.

Standing Elk sat still, his piercing brown eyes watching, ready to catch the slightest breath of movement. His village was two days away in the foothills to the northeast. Since leaving, his raiding party had encountered no other human beings. His warriors were growing restless. They followed him because he had a sixth sense for finding and successfully engaging the enemy. If and when he ever lost that, they would follow someone else. He needed to decide if he should lead his warriors farther south and hope he found an enemy to raid or simply head back to their village, hunting along the way.

Standing Elk had lived for forty summers. Many years before, while hunting with his father, he had seen Spanish soldiers from a distance. The Spaniards had been riding horses, and two of them had carried rifles. His first real encounter with the Spanish had come years later when he had been in a raiding party farther south of the normal hunting grounds. They had attempted to ambush several Spanish soldiers, but, at the last moment, a dog had alerted the soldiers to their presence. The soldiers had escaped in the ensuing skirmish.

One of their warriors, Little Bear, had been shot and wounded. Since that time, Standing Elk had sought out the Spanish or anyone who had horses or rifles. Those items represented power and strength. He wondered why he thought of that now. He decided to take one more careful scan of the horizon.

Suddenly, he saw a flicker of movement out of the corner of his eye far away in Tahosa Valley. He froze, keeping his eyes locked on the last place they had rested, waiting for more movement.

It was almost a full minute until he saw something move again out of the corner of his eye, far down and away to the south of the Valley. Because of the clarity of the day, he recognized a small herd of elk coming out of a stand of trees and into a meadow. He counted six.

He relaxed a little, disappointed. Game could easily be found closer to their village; he had hoped to see men.

Idly watching as the small herd of elk continued to make their way farther into the Valley, he saw them suddenly look up from their grazing, face south as if on cue, and then turn and run north. A moment later six Spanish soldiers on horseback rode out of a stand of trees. The sun briefly reflected off the first soldier's helmet.

Standing Elk could hardly believe his eyes. He squinted a little, looking harder. What an omen! The elk was his namesake; he had been given powerful medicine. He watched the small group for a few minutes as he formulated a plan. When he knew what needed to be done, he made a marmot call that alerted his warriors. He showed them the Spaniards and told them the plan he had crafted. They mounted their horses and made their way in a single file down to the head of Tahosa Valley.

———⟫●⟪———

As Captain Hernandez and his men rode out of the stand of trees, his thoughts were on returning to Santa Fe as quickly as possible once the mission was accomplished. He sat erect in the saddle. The last several days since leaving Santa Fe had been uneventful. He and his men were on an expedition to explore for mineral sites and to report on the lay of the land.

Officials had heard about an area with several square miles of parks and meadows far to the north. Since not very much was known about it, Hernandez had orders to make a detailed exploration and report his findings.

Hernandez was more comfortable in town than in the wilderness. He liked to be around his fellow officers, not the ragtag enlisted men he had been leading for weeks. The contempt he felt for them was returned in equal measure.

And it was the men who followed him who were becoming more and more concerned the farther north they moved. The Utes were bad enough, but the stories they had heard of the Arapahos made them anxious. They did not want to have a run in with them—especially with a man like Hernandez in the lead.

The only hitch they had encountered so far was when they had broken camp that morning. Sergeant Jimenez had encountered load problems with two of the three packhorses. Impatiently, the captain had ordered Jimenez to give the third packhorse to one of the soldiers, fix the problems, and catch up with them. The fact that he had not waited for Jimenez and had split the party only added to the men's anxiety.

Hernandez was the third born son of a wealthy aristocrat. He held his title because of his father's position, and with the title came the opportunity for fame and fortune. He had only recently arrived from Mexico City with no field experience, believing that Indians were no threat to well trained soldiers. He also had great faith in armor to protect him and his men in any kind of assault. Unfortunately, he had never witnessed the fighting skill of an Indian warrior in his own element; if he had, he would have taken greater caution.

⟶⬥⟵

Sergeant Jimenez had not been having a good morning. He was not an overly superstitious man, but he still wondered why the girth strap on one packsaddle and a pannier strap on the other packhorse had chosen to break at the same time. The arrogance and inexperience of Hernandez only heightened the uneasy feeling he had in the pit of his stomach, and any haste only seemed to slow him down. Despite the coolness of the morning, Jimenez was wiping beads of sweat off his forehead.

Finally the repairs were complete. He was twenty minutes behind the main party when he started out. Unlike the captain, Jimenez had survived several skirmishes with Indians. The only protection within five hundred miles was with the main party and the weapons they carried. He pushed his packhorses with a sense of urgency to catch up.

Near the upper end of Tahosa Valley, along the stream, lay a marsh several hundred yards wide and about a mile long. There was some solid ground but mostly areas where a man could sink up to his knees in mud. Several small, seasonal streambeds also traced their ways through the marsh, giving a man plenty of places to hide. A game trail followed the only solid ground close to the stream. Toward the head of the valley and near present day Aspen Lodge, the marsh began to thin out and then end.

Five minutes later, the main party of soldiers entered the south end of the marsh following the game trail. Hernandez was irritated by the uneven and boggy ground the trail crossed. After several minutes of tedious travel his only thought was getting back to firm ground.

As Hernandez came abreast of a downed pine tree, he heard the shrill cry of a wounded rabbit. It was the last sound he ever heard. One arrow pierced his neck, and another hit him just under his right armpit. The battle was over swiftly with only one soldier firing off a wild shot.

⟶►◄⟵

Jimenez was several hundred yards from the marsh when he heard the battle cries and the lone rifle shot. He stopped to listen, his body tense, the uneasy feeling in his gut mixing with fear. When he saw the packhorse running from the marsh, he turned east and headed toward the west side of present day Twin Sisters Mountain. He reasoned that going up on to the mountain and not staying in the valley would help confuse any pursuit.

He had been gone for several minutes when the two warriors came out of the marsh following the tracks of the packhorse. Unfortunately for Jimenez, the spooked packhorse smelled his horses and started to follow them. As soon as the warriors saw the other tracks, they stopped and studied them. The older warrior motioned to the other to head back and inform Standing Elk, while he continued to follow Jimenez and the three packhorses.

Jimenez was in trouble, and he knew it. He had gotten past the clenching fear in his gut; the adrenaline was now pumping through his veins. After crossing Tahosa Creek, he soon topped out on to a small ridge and stopped to give his horses a breather. He heard a horse coming up behind him and whipped around. It was the same packhorse he had seen coming out of the marsh during the fight. He did not have much time.

Jimenez had no illusions that he could outrun the war party. He had to think fast and find a position from which to make a stand. Looking through an opening in the trees, he saw a large rock outcropping resembling a man's thumb farther up the mountain. That would at least give him a defensible position.

It took him several minutes of hard riding to get to the thumb's base. On the north side, a small stream surfaced for several dozen yards then went back underground. The grass was tall and lush around the stream. Jimenez dismounted and kneeled down to get a drink of water. The horses spread out and drank as well. He cupped his hand and lifted the water to his mouth, listening for the sound of his enemy's pursuit. The water was cool and clear, but he did not notice. His eyes were too busy scanning his surroundings.

As he looked around, he saw a hole in the rock just under a low overhang in front of him. The only way to see it was at his present location. He went over and kneeled down to inspect the hole. It was actually an opening into a cave. The watercourse had at one time flowed this way and hollowed out the area. He crawled in and found himself in a room. It was too dark to see the actual size, but he sensed it was large. He had found his way of escape!

He immediately went back out, stripped the packs from the packhorses and the saddle and bridle from his mount. He threw the equipment and packs into the cave. He then took the horses further up the hillside and loosely tied them behind a small stand of aspens. He ran back down to the cave entrance, taking a quick look around to see that no items were left outside the cave. The horse and his tracks were all indistinguishable from one another, so the Indians would have a hard time figuring out what he had done. Satisfied, he quickly crawled back into the cave. Thirty seconds later the Indian tracker came around the base of the rock outcropping, saw the stream, and stopped.

Soon the main war party caught up to the tracker, who was standing near the stream, confused by the jumble of tracks. Standing Elk was concerned. He immediately sent two warriors to the rock outcropping to act as guards while the other warriors spread out to look for signs. It took only a few minutes for one of the warriors to signal he had found a trail heading farther up the mountain. They soon found the four horses.

Keeping four warriors as guards over their current possessions, Standing Elk took the rest of his band and fanned out on foot to search for tracks. After several minutes of searching, they were only able to find the tracks of Jimenez heading back down the mountain and into the stream. They lost his tracks there.

Standing Elk signaled for his warriors to re-group. As they gathered, he could see the eagerness in their eyes to find Jimenez.

"I know he is close," one of the warriors said through gritted teeth. "I can feel it."

"I feel it, too, but there is a storm coming," Standing Elk said, motioning to the menacing thunderheads. "We will continue the search until it reaches us. Once the rain comes, any signs will be gone. If we find him before the rain comes, good. If not, we will return to our village with what we have won and not be ashamed."

The band dispersed again. The storm steadily moved closer as the warriors searched. Finally torrential rain caused the mountain side to run with water, wiping away all evidence of Jimenez. Standing Elk and his warriors ended their search and turned toward home.

CHAPTER 3

Hearing the Indians outside, Jimenez stealthily moved his belongings to the darkest corner of the cave and positioned himself with rifle in hand. Fatigue, chills, and hunger gnawed at his body, but fear of knowing what awaited him if caught alive kept him focused on the immediate danger.

Strength came from gripping his issued rifle and knowing the dagger, which his father gave him as a gift long ago, was strapped to his leg. Lightning, rolling thunder, and pounding rain outside the cave entrance told him that a storm was passing overhead. The rhythmic noise of the downpour slowly eased his tension and Jimenez drifted off into a deep sleep.

Awakening with a jolt to deathly silence, Jimenez listened. The storm was gone, but were the Indians? After creeping to the entrance of the cave to peer out, he could see no one and only heard the blue jays chattering. Cautiously he ventured out. Discovering he was alone, he went to check on his horses. They were gone! He was truly alone with no way out but to walk.

"I must always be vigilant. My enemies may return at any time," Jimenez vowed to himself.

Once back in the cave on that first morning alone, he lit a candle and inspected his new dwelling. The room was about twenty feet long by ten feet wide. The ceiling was about eight feet high and very uneven and had a large crack on one side that allowed in a bit of light. This would make a good chimney for a fire. He then turned and saw the old stream course. The dry streambed followed the lower side of the cave wall and then went down into a natural tunnel that headed back into the mountain. He decided to follow it.

The floor of the tunnel was littered with chunks of rock that had fallen from the ceiling. The air was stale and cool. After several minutes of following the tunnel, slowly descending into the mountain, he realized that candlelight was reflecting off a small quartz vein that was running along the ceiling.

As he went further along, the tunnel turned and headed further down into the mountain. As the tunnel widened, the quartz vein also widened. Suddenly Jimenez stopped dead in his tracks. He held the candle up higher. The vein was now laced with gold!

He stood transfixed for a moment then continued walking very slowly. He discovered that at five hundred yards the tunnel took a very steep decent deeper into the mountain and that it also widened so that the roof became several feet high. At that point, the tunnel became like a chute heading straight down into the depths of the mountain and the black unknown. By this point, the quartz vein was completely gold.

"Well, I'll be…" Jimenez exclaimed softly, under his breath.

His voice sounded strange in the tunnel, echoing off the walls, getting lost in the darkness below. With only the single candle, he could not see how long the steep portion of the tunnel extended, but his instincts told him it had great depth.

He was overwhelmed. He sat down and put his head in his hands. Suddenly, he began to laugh. He saw the irony of it all. If it had not been for two packsaddle straps breaking, he would be dead with the rest of his fellow soldiers. Now he was still alive but holed up in a cave, sitting beneath a vein of gold with no way to carry it out.

Jimenez had lived a hard life, and a Spanish enlisted soldier's pay was very little. He was used to doing without. Now, just several feet away, was more gold than most men would see in a lifetime. How could he get the gold out of the tunnel and himself out of the mountains with it?

After several minutes, he realized his candle was burning low. He went back to the main cave, sat down, and began to think about his priorities. The first order of business would be to make a fire pit below the natural chimney and then take stock of his supplies. There was several months of food if augmented with fresh meat. He must trap game and collect wood far away from the cave so there would be no evidence of him living there. He also must put a section of tarp over the entrance to keep animals out and the heat inside.

He had a shovel, a pick, a good axe, and several dozen candles, but would need to find beeswax to make more. He had twine wrapped around various packages of supplies to use for wicks. It would require many more candles to have enough light to work in the chute to mine the gold.

Over the next several days, Jimenez gathered firewood and trapped small game. On his second day out of the cave, he found a large hollow, dead pine that yielded several pounds of beeswax for candles. A week after finding the cave, he made himself go down to the battle site. The day was slightly overcast, and the breeze was cooler. There was a foretaste of winter in the air that only added to the somberness of his mission.

It took Jimenez most of the day to bury the remains of his fellow soldiers in a common grave. When he was finished, loneliness crept over him. He shook it off and turned back to the mountain. He saw only tracks of animals in the area and no signs of Indians, which helped him feel more secure. He must be extra vigilant.

Jimenez formulated a plan to mine the gold. He needed to build platforms in the chute to reach the gold vein. That day he found a stand of Lodge Pole pines to fell for his lumber. Over the next several weeks, he began the backbreaking work of cutting trees down in such a way that the stumps were below the ground. He then stacked them in the tunnel leading to the chute. From the branches, he made several dozen long pegs to use as nails to secure the poles together for the platforms. He also gathered in a winter firewood supply.

Jimenez worked nonstop for thirty days before he was ready to begin making extra candles and the platforms. He had developed a daily routine of getting up with the sun, waking up with a cold splash of frigid stream water on his face, and eating a quick breakfast before heading out to bring in his lumber.

It did not take much of a fire to cook and keep the cave warm. The crack allowed the smoke out and dissipated it to the point where it was invisible. The flap of canvas over the entrance helped to conceal the opening and also keep the elements out. Jimenez's cave was secure, warm, and comfortable living quarters.

At the end of October, he awoke to snow falling. He stood inside the cave entrance, watching the large flakes come down, contemplating his chute-making project.

He had decided on three platforms, each twenty feet long and six feet wide. They would be anchored into the steep slope of the chute by posts. The last and lowest platform would be sixteen feet below the first. He would need to use a rope to anchor himself while he dug the holes for the supporting posts.

While in the chute planning the platforms, a large chunk of quartz fell from the ceiling and rolled down a long way before it splashed into some water below. The blackness at the bottom caused chills to run down his spine. He knew his life and fortune depended on careful and deliberate planning. During construction, he would have to watch his step so he did not end up at the bottom of the chute. He went back to the main cave, began to fix breakfast, and decided that the following day he would be ready to start construction.

Jimenez built the ladders and platforms over a two-month period. The most time-consuming part was drilling out holes for the pegs to join the logs together. He needed strong platforms to hold his weight and the weight of the rock he would be taking off the ceiling. He was constantly dodging falling debris from the unstable ceiling as he worked and was thankful the day the platforms were completed and he was ready to mine the gold.

Jimenez was careful by nature, so he gave much thought to his mining plan. He determined to collect rock for two hours each day and spend the rest of the time separating the gold by the fire in his cave. He decided that once he had collected one hundred pounds of gold he would stop. When he walked out in the spring, he would take ten pounds with him and come back for the rest with horses. A man walking out of the wilderness with gold would draw attention, but he had all winter to think about a solution to that problem.

On the first day of mining, he pulled down fifty pounds of rock. He hauled it up to the cave and extracted what he guessed was ten ounces of gold. He used a crude scale to weigh the separated gold.

Long, tedious days passed like this, and Jimenez was becoming a different man. The strain of working under the constant threat of danger was taking its toll. He talked out loud to himself, and his hands continually shook. His beard was scraggly and his clothes unkempt. His eyesight was strained because of the limited light.

"It's been twenty days working on this rock," Jimenez muttered to himself. He was on the edge of the upper platform. "Twenty days. Or has it? Maybe longer…" He lifted his pick and wielded it for what seemed like the thousandth time.

"I can't keep track anymore. The days all run together." He wielded his pick again. "Everything runs together."

He was still muttering when several hundred pounds of the rock ceiling began to give way.

"Oh, dear God!" Jimenez screamed.

The bulk of the rock struck him on the head and shoulder before damaging the platform and then tumbling off into the darkness of the chute. Jimenez was knocked on his back onto the second platform, unconscious.

Many hours passed before his eyelids fluttered opened. He was in total darkness. It took him a moment to remember where he was. His legs were dangling off the edge over the abyss. The back of his head felt like it had been split in two. He could not feel his left shoulder and arm. He suddenly became violently sick, and his only thought before passing out was, "Dear God, help me!"

When he awoke again, the darkness was like a shroud. He knew the truth: he was going to die. He felt it in the pit of his stomach. That same feeling of fear he had during the Indian attack was now mixed with certainty. He had never been a praying man nor thought much about God. But now he prayed, asking God to forgive him and give him strength to get back up the ladders to the main cave before he died. He did not want to die in the dark.

It took a long time to get back up the ladder. Then he began to make his way by feeling the edges of the tunnel. He felt the blood dripping down the side of his face. The tunnel seemed so long and dark. He kept repeating desperate prayers that he would be able to make it to the cave.

At last he was in the room that had provided him safety from his enemies and had become his home. He pulled his way to the fireplace and rested his head on his arm. He was thankful he would not die in the darkness of the tunnel. He pleaded with his Maker one last time, "Dear God, help me!" and then Jimenez died.

CHAPTER 4

LATE SUMMER 1968

Jack, Ben, and Jeb made their way through the warm, pine-scented forest. When they had left that morning with their knapsacks and their faithful black lab, Shadow, it had been cool. It was close to noon and warm now as they neared the outcropping they called the Thumb. It had a thick base and slowly rose to a rounded point against the deep-blue sky. Earlier, Jeb had seen the Thumb and suggested they do some exploring around it. They were all up to the challenge.

"Ben, let's find a good way to reach the top of the point," Jack suggested. The two boys took off while Jeb's curiosity led him down a trickling stream that was near the Thumb. Shadow recognized Jeb's susceptibility to danger and stayed with him, running ahead of him as they followed the stream.

"Sometimes you just have to take the road less traveled, Shadow," Jeb said to the lab. She wagged her tail in answer. "You never know what you might find."

Jeb stopped and knelt down to get a drink. He stood and readjusted his knapsack, stepped back a foot or two, and leaped across the stream. The soft edge of the opposite bank began to crumble under his feet, and he rolled forward, landing on all fours, losing his glasses in the process. He froze, hesitant to stand up and risk stepping on his glasses.

"Shadow, help me," he said to the black blur over to his right. "They couldn't have gone far."

Shadow sniffed around, trying her best to be useful. Jeb sighed with relief when his fingers brushed his glasses. He slipped his glasses back on, settling them over his ears, but his right eye was still blurry.

"Blast! The right lens is missing," he muttered. Back down on his knees, he felt through the carpet of pine needles and kini-kinic. Shadow dutifully continued sniffing around, finally barked, nosing something.

"Good job, girl! You found it!" Jeb ruffled her ears. "You're the smartest dog in the world."

Shadow took his praise with a slight wag of her tail then continued sniffing, already onto a new scent. Jeb sat down on a rock to pop the lens back in his frame and then adjusted his glasses on his head. He saw clearly now, and his mouth fell open when Shadow came back into view.

She had a man's arm bone in her mouth! "S… somebody's arm," he stuttered as Shadow dropped it at his feet. "Jack! Ben!" Jeb's loud yells brought his brothers quickly.

"What on earth?" Jack and Ben came to stop beside Jeb, staring with wide eyes at Shadow.

"Where'd you get it, girl?" Jack asked. Shadow's tail wagged, and she glanced back upstream as if to say, "Just up that way." Jack met Ben's eyes and Ben nodded. They headed off, their eyes searching carefully along the stream.

"Hey! What do I do with this?" Jeb called after his brothers. He looked down at the arm bone, gave a shudder, then grabbed it and ran to catch up with Jack and Ben.

The three of them stopped abruptly as the stream disappeared into the ground. Intently they set off in three different directions searching for anything that might give them some idea of where the skeleton arm came from.

Jeb saw a flat rock, set the skeleton arm down on top of it, and wiped his hands on the sides of his pants. He cocked his head to one side, staring interestedly at it. How old was it? Where had it come from? Who had it belonged to?

Just then Ben called out. "I think I found something!" Jack and Jeb and Shadow were beside him in an instant. Ben was staring at a small entrance in a rocky outcropping.

"A cave?" Jack said in a low voice.

Before anyone could say anything else, Shadow disappeared into the black entrance. They stood silent, waiting, wondering if they should follow. They heard her padding around on the gravel floor inside, blowing loudly through her nostrils at the musty interior. Suddenly she returned with a leg bone in her mouth. Her tail was wagging with the excitement of her newest find.

"Oh, boy." Ben swallowed hard. "I'm not sure if we should go in…"

Jeb shook off the chill of apprehension that had fallen over the three of them. "We've got to," he said with determination. He plunged forward with Shadow at his side, but Jack quickly pulled him back.

"Wait. Ben's right. We have to think about this first."

Jeb shook his arm free from his brother's grasp. "What's to think about? We have to go in and find out what's in there," he insisted.

"Okay, I want to go in too, but let's be smart about it at least." Jack swung his pack around and pulled out a couple of stick matches. "I'll go in first." He looked over at Jeb. "You follow Ben and Shadow and bring up the rear."

Jack went over to the entrance, stooped down, and took a deep breath. "Keep your heads down, and get out fast if I say so." They followed him slowly and waited for him to light the match. The entrance was narrow, but the flickering light revealed a wide cavern. As they stood mesmerized, Shadow trotted right over to the rest of the skeleton. Next to the skeleton was a Spanish helmet, dull now with age, but amazing still for its workmanship. Their eyes widened in amazement as they scanned the cavern wall.

On the other side of the remains were bags of gold, one spilled over on its side so that some of the nuggets lay in the gravel beside it. Scanning further along the wall, there was a small dagger in its sheath, a musket, powder horn, and a whole collection of other items that were all well preserved because of the cool, dry climate.

Jack waved out the remainder of the stick match, as it was about to burn his fingers. The chill darkness of the cave took over for a moment until he struck the next one. The resuming light was welcome, and they breathed a sigh of relief, turning their eyes back to their discovery. The three of them squatted, staring for several more moments, not saying anything. Even Shadow sat beside them as if she understood the significance of the moment.

"That's gold, isn't it?" whispered Jeb.

"Uh, huh," Jack whispered back.

Ben just shook his head and then let out a breath he had been holding for too long. The stick match was burning steadily, and there was only one left. Shadows were lengthening outside the entrance. They could see the sunlight growing dimmer.

"We have a ways to go to get home by dark, and Mom wants us home for dinner," Ben said finally.

"Sure. You're right." Jack shook himself. "Okay. Let's take the helmet, the dagger, and one of the gold nuggets," he said as if he had been thinking about it.

"Gosh," Jeb whispered as Ben handed him the dagger. Jack took the helmet, and Ben safeguarded the gold nugget in his front button-down shirt pocket.

"Okay. Let's go," Jack instructed. As he turned away, he caught a funny look on Ben's face. He looked back to see why. There was a tunnel that led right into the mountain!

"Look at the tools. He must have been mining," Ben said, pointing to the opposite wall of the cave.

"You're probably right, but we've got to go," Jack replied, holding up the dwindling stick match. Jack waved out the stick match before it reached his fingers, and the two of them joined Jeb and Shadow, already outside the entrance. Stepping out into the fresh air was a relief, and they were eager to reach home.

Hiking down the mountain, they were quiet for most of the way, lost in their own thoughts. When they were about five minutes from home, Jack quietly suggested, "Let's just keep this to ourselves for now. The gold and the cave, I mean. We can tell Mom and Dad about the helmet and the dagger. But until we know that nugget is really gold, let's not say anything about it."

Ben and Jeb didn't argue with Jack's idea of deception but made suggestions of their own. "Maybe we could get Mom or Dad to drive us to the library so we can do some research and find out for sure," Ben said.

"And let's go back to the cave soon to do more exploring," Jeb added.

Jack nodded in agreement. "Sure! We can bring flashlights and candles and more supplies so we can take our time and find out exactly where that tunnel leads."

CHAPTER 5

The brothers made it home right at dinnertime. Over the meal, they shared with their parents their interesting find. Jeb could barely keep his seat at the dinner table. All their eyes were shining, even Ben's, although he didn't say much, just watched as Royal looked over the helmet and the dagger. Sara was the one asking questions, trying to pull together all the pieces of her sons' hurried narrative.

"So," Jack said, "we want to go to the library and look these things up and see what information we can fin—"

"To try and solve the mystery," Jeb added. He looked at his dad. "Can we, Dad?"

"Your mom will have to take you, but I don't see why not. It definitely is something to research. I'll be interested to see what you find."

The three boys turned to their mother, and she assured them she would take them on Monday when she needed to go into town for some groceries.

That night while they lay in their bunk beds, the boys planned their return trip to the cave. The start of school was only a week away, so they would have to go before then. They felt guilty about not telling their parents about the gold, but they had all come to the same conclusion: they wanted to figure out if it was really gold and then they would tell their parents. There was no need to cause excitement if it wasn't real in the first place.

Monday finally came. They headed for Estes Park right after breakfast. Sara was determined that the boys get haircuts. She dropped them off at the barbershop near the Village Theater, which was across the street from Bond Park, the library, and the police station. After they did their research at the library, the boys planned to walk up to the Tender Steer for lunch. Sara would pick them up there.

The brothers raced each other to the library after their haircuts. Jack assigned Ben to investigate the gold while he explored the background of the helmet and dagger. Jeb followed along with Ben, more interested in the gold. The three of them ended up at a table in the back of the library with several books a piece.

Jeb went back and forth between the two of them, hanging over their arms. "Have you found a picture of gold yet, Ben?" Jeb asked impatiently, forgetting he was in a library. "How much do you think those bags are worth?"

Ben looked up, holding his finger to his lips. "Shhh! For the last time, Jeb, do you want the whole world to know?" he said in a stern whisper.

⟫●⟪

John Holt had been watching the boys from the moment they entered. He had come to the library to borrow money from his half sister who worked as a librarian, but she had turned him down flat. "Get going and leave me alone," she told him.

As he was leaving, the boys had hurriedly entered the library. He heard Jeb mention the word *gold* as they went by and he decided to follow them. He was a tall man with broad shoulders and dark hair. He was surprisingly clean-shaven and had a light colored scar over his right eye. He twisted a stained Stetson in his hands.

Holt was frequently in trouble with the law, a person others purposely avoided. He had just been released from jail for poaching elk. Although he was quiet, he was like a gun half-cocked, ready to go off at any time. His eyes never left the boys as he followed them.

⟫●⟪

The boys' appetites pushed them to check out their books and head over to the Tender Steer for lunch. Once they had their food, Ben looked across at Jack and said, "Okay, what did you find?"

"Well, they're definitely Spanish. The dagger is," Jack replied.

Jeb was leaning with his elbows on the table, listening eagerly, forgetting the grilled cheese sandwich in front of him. "And the helmet?" he interjected excitedly.

"Yes, the helmet, too. It was worn by soldiers…a *sallet* helmet is what it's called."

"Wow." Jeb whistled under his breath.

"It could be hundreds of years old," Jack finished. He looked at Ben. "What did you find?"

Ben opened one of the books and slid it across the table to Jack. "I think it's real. See, real gold is bright yellow like what we found. It doesn't look the same as the stuff you see in jewelry. Pure gold is too soft, so they mix it with other metals to give it strength. The stuff we found is pretty soft."

"It does look like the picture," Jack agreed. Jeb pulled at the book, wanting to see the picture for himself.

After a few more minutes, they stopped talking and ate, thinking about their next step. They decided to ask their parents if they could spend Friday night and Saturday up at Lost Cabin in the vicinity of the Thumb. That would be their excuse to take the horses and extra supplies they would need to explore the cave. It would not be an outright lie, but they knew it was not the whole truth. They did plan to bring home the gold though, and then their parents would know everything.

Jack paid the bill when he saw their mom coming up the street, and the boys hurried out to the station wagon. All three of them began to tell their mom about the dagger and the helmet, being careful not to mention the gold. They were so caught up in their conversation, they didn't realize the stranger from the library had followed them to the Tender Steer and was now following far behind them in a Dodge Power Wagon.

Holt could follow the Talons at a safe distance and not worry about losing them because Highway 7 had no major turn-offs. When the Talons pulled in to their driveway, he pulled off the highway and pondered what to do next. He decided to stay hidden, follow the boys' every move, and try to discover their secret gold stash. They were hiding gold. He could feel it.

He watched them for several days, only going back to his apartment at night when he knew the family had gone to bed. This also gave him a chance to observe Royal Talon. Holt realized the boys' father would make a formidable adversary and wanted to avoid any chance of tangling with him.

His patience paid off Friday morning when he spied the boys leaving with horses, their black lab, and camping gear. Holt cautiously followed them, knowing the dog had a good nose and would alert the boys to his presence.

The day was warm, but there was a feel of autumn in the air. The Ponderosa pines gave off a familiar vanilla scent, the aspen leaves rustled in the breeze and a woodpecker made its rhythmic noise from somewhere nearby. The boys were grateful to be in the woods again and on their own.

It took them a couple hours of steady travel to get to the Thumb. Once there, they picketed the horses on long lead lines with halters so that they could eat and drink while the boys explored.

They had come well prepared to spend the night. Their knapsacks were filled with slickers, rope, matches, food, candles, flashlights, and extra batteries. Lost Cabin was only about a mile down the hill on a small ridge, but for now they took their knapsacks, sleeping bags, and saddles and placed them just inside the cave entrance.

With flashlights shedding plenty of light in the cave, they slowly looked at the skeleton, the old supplies, and the bags of gold. Shadow stood beside them, just as transfixed.

"Once we're done exploring the tunnel," Jack finally said, "we'll carry out what we can and tell Mom and Dad everything." The three of them felt the burden of deception, even as small and inconsequential as it seemed. Their revelation of the helmet and dagger had seemed to be enough at the time, but now as they faced the entrance of the underground tunnel, something told them it had not been nearly enough at all. The gloomy atmosphere vanished when Ben started forward into the tunnel.

"Let's see where it leads," he said firmly. The fact that the words and accompanying action were totally uncharacteristic of the quiet, cautious Ben drew the other two brothers after him. If Ben was okay with it, they were too. Besides, it was just a tunnel. They would find out where it led, explore anything it contained, head back out, and perhaps—just perhaps—find more gold. That thought alone started the adrenaline pumping through their veins and propelled them all forward into the dark hole of the tunnel.

As the boys ventured forward, a damp coldness pressed around them. Their flashlight beams bounced off the rough walls, casting shadows, causing even Shadow to walk slowly and cautiously. As they passed a stack of old candles, Jack and Ben both picked up a couple of handfuls and put them into their knapsacks. Jeb stared down the tunnel, straining his eyes to see, lost in the curiosity of what they would find at the end.

The darkness became thicker, and their flashlights had a difficult time dispelling it. Jeb shivered and grasped his flashlight harder. The tunnel gradually began to widen, and for the first time, they noticed a vein of quartz running through the ceiling above them. Jack swung the beam of his flashlight up and studied it as they continued slowly on.

There were pick marks and small specks of gold laced throughout the quartz. After a hundred more feet, they came to a roughly made platform. Jack held up his hand, and the three of them stopped, Shadow beside them. All three of them shined their flashlights down into the dark space below. There were two other platforms with ladders connecting them. Jack let out a soft whistle.

"Gosh," Jeb said under his breath. The light revealed a vein of quartz, very wide now and thick with gold.

"Jeb, you wait here with Shadow while Ben and I make sure the platforms are safe," Jack said. He stepped onto the ladder of the first platform with Ben shining his flashlight down. Ben followed him. They noticed damage had been done to the middle platform, although it felt secure under their feet. With confidence, Jack continued down to the last platform.

"Ben, help Jeb and Shadow to get down here. It seems safe to me. I'll give you some light," Jack said as he aimed his flashlight upward.

Once they all were on the lowest platform, Ben pointed his flashlight down the rest of the tunnel. "Wow! It's steep, Jack," Ben exclaimed. Jack was beside him then.

"It's too steep to keep going," Jack said.

"I'm not afraid…" Jeb interjected, but Jack held up his hand.

"Shhh. Listen."

The three of them stood in silence, listening hard, and even Shadow's ears perked up as she caught the sound. It was the sound of rushing water, far below. "Is it an underground stream?" Ben asked quietly.

"Must be, but we're not going to try to find out." Jack turned back to the middle platform. "At least not now. We would need more rope than we have to repel to the bottom." Ben had turned back with him. Jeb and Shadow still sat listening, looking down the vast deepness of the tunnel.

"Sure. Maybe we should go back up and do some more exploring in the main cavern. We can always come back down here later on. Maybe with Dad…" Suddenly a light shone down on them from the top platform. Four pairs of eyes blinked in the blinding light. Who…?

"Hello, boys! Fancy meeting you here."

CHAPTER 6

Shadow growled menacingly. Jeb started to say something, but Jack shushed him. The man flashed the light up to the top of the tunnel to inspect the vein of gold and let out a long, slow whistle. He then flashed it back into their eyes. "I should introduce myself," the man said. "My name is John Holt. I've been following you boys ever since I saw you in the library. I knew you had a secret. So now, I'd like to meet you face-to-face. Get up here. We need to talk."

When the boys made no answer and no move to start back up the platforms, Holt yelled impatiently, "Get up here *now!*"

"We're not going anywhere," Jack whispered fiercely to his brothers. Ben's eyes were large; he gulped and swallowed. Jeb's mouth was pursed, his eyes narrowed, his hands in defiant fists by his sides. Shadow was growling deep in her throat.

"We're not going anywhere," Jack said, loudly this time, as firmly as he could. "And my dad is coming up to the cave soon, so you'd better leave us alone."

The man snorted. "Huh! You're dad isn't within ten miles of here. Didn't your parents teach you not to fib? I saw your horses and sleeping bags. I bet you didn't even tell your parents you were coming to the cave."

Even while he was talking the wheels were turning in Holt's mind. If he could somehow get rid of the boys, he could make sure no one ever found the cave entrance, and he would have all the gold.

"Quit trying my patience, boys, and get up here," he roared. But the boys did not move.

Jack tried to stand tall and put on a brave front so that Ben and Jeb would not be afraid, but inside he was shaking with fear. Ben knew Jack was just as afraid as he was, but Jeb, on the other hand, looked as though he might try to take Holt on single-handedly. Shadow was with Jeb.

"Okay...if you won't come up to me, I'll just come down to you!"

Jack put his hand on his hunting knife secured in a sheath attached to his belt. Ben did the same, pushing Jeb behind him. As Holt put one foot on the ladder to the middle platform, Shadow lunged and began barking ferociously. Undeterred, Holt settled his full weight on the ladder, causing a main log brace to give away from the wall. The middle platform began to sag and tilt into the platform below where the boys stood staring in wide-eyed terror. Within seconds, the supports to all three platforms gave out, causing them to move as one. Holt lunged wildly for the ladder just as the platforms slowly began slipping backward down the steep slope of the tunnel.

"Ben! Jeb! Lay down flat and hold on!" Jack yelled. He grabbed Shadow and flattened himself over her, his fingertips gripping the logs. The platforms picked up speed and careened down the slope. Flashlight beams randomly bounced off the tunnel walls in the darkness. Holt was above them, yelling profanities. The boys clung to the platform as it crashed into the sides of the tunnel on its speedy descent.

Holt's yelling became muffled, and motion seemed to slow. Jack struggled to hold on to Shadow, wondering if he would need to make the choice to let her go in order to save his life. The tunnel narrowed, and the slope turned vertical. The platforms, too wide for the tunnel, began to stack up until they came to a sudden, crashing stop.

The boys catapulted downward with rocks, dirt, and shattered portions of the platform. Their landing—at the bottom of a much larger tunnel—was softened by a shallow pool of water. In a few moments, the last bits of dust and debris stopped raining down around them.

Holt's deafening screams of pain echoed off the tunnel walls. He was pinned in the wreckage.

Ben was on his hands and knees with his eyes closed, praying the screaming would stop. He opened his eyes—not to complete darkness—but saw a murky light glowing a few feet to his right. He crawled over and discovered one of the flashlights underwater. His rejoicing was cut short as a searing pain shot through his left hand. The flashlight revealed a dislocated finger.

Movement to his right alerted him to Jeb. He was alive even though he was moaning in pain. Scanning the tunnel slowly revealed Jack lying on his back, unconscious in the shallow water across from Jeb. Ben clumsily splashed over and lifted him to a sitting position. With blood oozing from a gash on his forehead, Jack's eyes fluttered open. Relief flooded Ben.

"Are you okay?" Ben asked. Jack nodded, dazed. Shadow splashed through the water toward them, looking as though she had come through the ordeal better than any of them. Jeb slowly made his way next to them, holding his right arm as if it were in a sling, feeling his way with the other.

"My collarbone is broke," he said in a matter-of-fact tone. He had broken both of them before. "Oh, and I lost my glasses."

The trio sat in the silence realizing Holt's screams had stopped. Ben shone his flashlight upward to the pile of debris caught in the tunnel several yards up. The passage was completely blocked by the crushed platforms, including Holt's mangled body pinned in the wreckage.

Ben let the flashlight fall to his lap, and their eyes met. Having regained his senses, Jack took charge. He had each one of them take stock of their supplies. They had their knapsacks still on, but all the contents of Jack's knapsack had dumped out in the fall. They began to look around them, picking up anything they could find as they searched.

They worked in silence, afraid to say anything in the darkness of the tunnel. The shock of what had happened was still fresh in their minds. The disaster, from beginning to end, continued to play over and over in their minds. Holt's screams still echoed in their ears.

They took a piece of rope from Jeb's knapsack and made a crude sling for his arm. Then Jack took a hold of Ben's injured finger and yanked as hard as he could.

"Hey!" Ben yelled. "That hurt!"

"I saw that once on *The Rifleman* show when Luke had to fix Mica's dislocated finger," Jack replied.

"Grrrreat," Ben moaned. Jack splinted Ben's injured finger to his index finger for support using some cloth strips from on old T-shirt in Ben's knapsack. Using the remnant of the T-shirt, Jack washed his own forehead with some water.

"Jeb's glasses." Jack motioned around them. "Let's try to find those first."

Jeb plopped down on a rock, holding his arm against him, pain shooting through his shoulder. He could barely see as it was, but in the dim light of the flashlight, he could see almost nothing. Jeb bent down to rinse his face, and as he scooped up a handful of water, his hand caught the arm of his glasses. "Yahoo! I found them!" he shouted. The lenses were scratched but still usable.

After that, they decided to light a candle and save the flashlight battery for when they would really need it. The only other flashlight they found had a smashed bulb and was useless. They had seven sets of batteries, and Jack figured they would last about two hours each. They took stock of their other supplies: an airtight tin of kitchen matches, a dozen candles, their hunting knives, slickers, and food for a few days.

"What now?" Ben asked as if he hoped the answer would echo back to them from the depths of the tunnel.

"I think we should pray," Jack replied. "It's a miracle we made it out of that alive."

They bowed their heads there in the underground tunnel, water up to their ankles, weary, dazed, and hurting. "Dear God, Thank You that we are alive. Please show us what to do now. Please protect us. We know how to be tough, Lord, but we need Your help. Please help us. Amen."

The silence that followed was deafening. The candlelight only faintly dispelled the dense blackness.

"I'm afraid," Jeb whispered hoarsely.

"We're all afraid," Jack answered. "But we're going to make it."

CHAPTER 7

"We can't go back up," Jack stated flatly. The tunnel opening was about fifteen yards above their heads, completely jammed with debris. Even if they had tools to move anything, it was likely the entire pileup would come down on top of them.

"Should we just wait for help to come?" Ben asked. Although none of them had a watch, they guessed that it had been a few hours since they had first entered the cave from above. It would be early afternoon now.

"We told Dad and Mom we'd be back tomorrow night. They won't start worrying until then," Jack replied. He was thinking hard. If they stayed where they were, they would eventually run out of candles and batteries. The thought of being left in the cold, dense darkness around them was more frightening than the thought of trying to find their way out on their own. "We're going to head upstream to search for a way out," Jack decided. He stood up and adjusted his knapsack. "Come on. Let's go."

They walked single file, Jack then Jeb then Ben, each holding onto the knapsack in front of them. Shadow picked her own path alongside them. Unbeknownst to the boys, the underground river where they found themselves was one hundred feet below the surface of Tahosa Creek. It ran south through Tahosa Valley flowing into Cabin Creek, finally flowing into the North St. Vrain River several miles away to the south. With few exceptions, the boys' river mimicked the path of Tahosa Creek on the surface.

The depth of the riverbed varied from three to twelve inches. Jack stepped up on the rocks instead of slogging through the water although it made for slow going. His candle did little to scatter the darkness, making their steps that much more hazardous.

As time passed, the size of the riverbed continued to shrink. When they reached the end of the riverbed, which opened into an underground spring, it was clear they could go no further. Suddenly the candle went out, and the oppressive darkness enveloped the three boys.

"Can either of you see light anywhere?" Jack asked, his voice tense. Seeing the answer for himself, he quickly relit the candle and made his way around his brothers, heading back the way they had come. Their discouragement was great. To go back the way they had come weighed on all of them, especially Jack. As the eldest, he felt a deep responsibility to get them out.

Slowly they made their way back to their starting point. Jeb was in a lot of pain from his collarbone but kept silent. "Our only option is to head downstream," Jack said quietly, pushing back the despair and panic he felt deep in his heart, knowing he needed to be brave for the sake of his brothers.

"Wait! Let's leave a note," Ben said. "We can write it on one of our lunch sacks and leave it where someone might find it." They agreed. Ben quickly wrote the note and pinned it under a small rock several yards downstream to keep it protected from a cave-in. Then they continued on.

If the boys could have seen their route from up above, it would have been like looking down a large water hose that was lying on the ground. There were rocks on the floor of the hose, and it twisted and turned, leaving few areas to walk except down the center.

"There's another one," Jeb blurted out.

"Another what?" Jack asked. Annoyed, he stopped and partially turned around. Then he saw it: a small watercourse flowing into the main tunnel.

"Let's put out the candle every time we reach one of these and look for light," Ben suggested. Jack blew out the candle. They stood in the darkness, silent. Shadow stood against Ben's legs. They were weary and sore and welcomed the chance to rest. But there was no light and not even a whisper of airflow. Jack relit the candle, and they continued on.

Three hours into their trek downstream, the tunnel narrowed and steadily descended. The falling slope and rising water made it harder to pick their way across the rocks. Soon they were soaked from slipping and falling. The river showed no signs of abating. Jack struggled to keep the candle lit. Jeb fell against a rock, hitting his injured shoulder and his cry of pain echoed against the walls of the tunnel.

Jack headed to a cluster of dry rocks and sat down, Ben and Jeb following. He opened his knapsack and distributed parts of a smashed peanut butter and jelly sandwich to his brothers, giving a few pieces to Shadow.

"At least we don't have to worry about getting thirsty," Jack said wryly. He held up the candle, and they could see the water moving among the rocks. Since coming through the rapids, they had descended fifty feet in elevation. Sitting in their wet clothes, they felt extremely cold. Jeb's teeth chattered as he sat with an arm around Shadow, whose thick coat repelled water well. She seemed to know he needed her to help keep warm.

Jack and Ben dug in their knapsacks, put on their slickers, and helped Jeb put on his. They huddled together with their backs against each other for extra warmth. Eventually they fell into a restless sleep, Shadow by their side.

While the boys slept, a huge storm began to build above them. Big clouds developed over Estes Cone and the north end of Tahosa Valley, moving southwest toward Longs Peak, Mount Lady Washington, and Mount Meeker. It was the kind of storm that anyone hiking through the boulder field on Longs Peak would never forget.

As the storm passed over Battle Mountain, it dropped several inches of rain in a few short hours. The first, small watercourses that the boys passed earlier carried water from Estes Cone and Battle Mountain and would soon swell to raging rivers.

Surely this is only a nightmare, Jeb thought as he slowly blinked open his eyes. Blackness! He involuntarily cried out as he realized it was reality. Jack and Ben were both jarred awake. There was some mumbling; then a match was struck and a candle lit.

"Are you okay?" Jack asked as he held the candle up.

"I'm fine. I just forgot where I was," Jeb replied.

"Me, too," Ben said. "You scared me to death."

Shadow was lapping the water. As Jack split another sandwich between them, he wondered how long they had slept.

"I wonder what Mom and Dad are doing…" Ben's voice trailed off.

"I'm still hungry," Jeb complained.

"Let's pray, and then we need to keep going," Jack said. They bowed their heads, Jack said a short prayer, and they continued on. They passed a watercourse on their left.

"Looks like that flows right from Twin Sisters," Jack said. They blew out the candle. No light. No movement of air. The candle was relit, and they continued on with heads down, trying their best to put one foot in front of the other. The slowly rising water and the tunnel's sudden, sharp, left turn went unnoticed by them all.

Sara Talon glanced out her kitchen window. Her hands were mechanically washing dishes, but her mind was on her sons. She awoke early that morning with a nagging thought that something was wrong.

"Oh, God, protect them," she prayed fervently. "Oh, God, keep them safe!"

Simultaneously, Royal paused outside the camp dining hall. He noticed the dark, menacing clouds hanging low over Longs Peak. A sense of foreboding stirred deep inside of him. He was normally very optimistic, but he could not shake the eerie feeling he had. *Dear God, please keep my boys safe*, he prayed.

The boys passed a large watercourse on their right. Once again there was no light, but there was some movement of air from the west tunnel when they relit the candle. This made them curious. "Hey, does it look like the water is rising and moving faster?" Jack anxiously asked Ben as they moved on ahead.

"Yeah, I noticed it too. Maybe it's raining up above," Ben replied. "It'd have to be a storm at the north end of the Valley for it to make a difference in the water level, right?"

"Yes, that's probably it." Jack looked at Jeb, who was being uncharacteristically quiet. Jack could tell he was in pain by the way his free hand clutched his slicker. Suddenly the water in the tunnel began to unmistakably rise as if a fire hydrant had just been opened into the riverbed above them. Even the air in the tunnel began to move, and Jack had to cup his hand around the candle's flame to keep it lit. Shadow's ears went up and the scruff on her back rose.

Hesitantly, they waded on as the water continued to rise. A sickening feeling rose in the pit of Jack's stomach. Shadow began to whine, expressing her concern that something was wrong. The river would soon be too high and swift for her to walk. Upstream, a strange new sound reached their ears. Jack stopped with Ben and Jeb beside him. Ben held Shadow's collar, patting her head.

"What's that noise?" Ben asked anxiously. The sound steadily grew in volume, like a distant roar of a freight train coming toward them down the track.

"Run!" Jack screamed. "Run back upstream!"

CHAPTER 8

Worse than any nightmare, they did not have the luxury of waking up to escape what was happening. They were trying to run, but the rising water and swift current impeded their legs, making their progress painfully slow. The once mysterious noise, now identified, pumped adrenaline through each one of them. Their reality was the roar of the rain-swollen western watercourse they recently passed upstream.

Jack stumbled over an unseen rock, and the candle was extinguished in the water.

"Quick, Ben, get my flashlight out of my knapsack!"

The roar was growing louder in the darkness. Ben hastily fumbled in Jack's knapsack.

"I can't find…" Ben fumbled some more. "Got it!" He turned it on and took the lead.

Jack grabbed Jeb, who was lagging behind in spite of his best efforts to keep up.

"I've got you, Jeb," he reassured his brother as he put Jeb's good arm around his neck to help him. Ben gripped

Shadow's collar, pulling her upstream in the swift current; the lab was valiantly paddling.

The roar was deafening now, and a stiff wind hit them as they came abreast of the western watercourse. Time slowed, and seconds felt like hours. Just as the three boys passed the entrance of the watercourse, a wall of water shot out the end like water from a fire hose, hitting the wall of the main tunnel with tremendous force that threatened to overtake them. The boys desperately fought their way upstream and out of the clutches of the water pouring from the mouth of the tunnel.

"It's no use!" Ben yelled, trying to keep the flashlight above water. "It's rising too fast!"

Jack gripped Jeb's collar, pulling him behind him. Shadow struggled to keep her head above the water as she paddled furiously. Desperation urged them forward. Panic rose in their throats. Jack didn't know what to do. There were no more options. His greatest fear since they first heard the roar was becoming a reality: they were all going to drown.

"Oh, God, help us!" Jack yelled out in desperation.

"Look!" Ben's cry was barely heard above the rushing of the water still filling the tunnel. "Over there!" He was pointing upstream. "There's a ledge above the water!" They all pushed for it with renewed hope, struggling against the water's pull. Shadow swam hard beside Ben, who soon reached the ledge and hoisted himself up. He lifted Shadow up by her collar.

The water was at Jack's chest and still rising. He boosted Jeb up to Ben, who struggled to lift his younger brother up on the ledge. Once he got him safely against the back wall, he reached back down for Jack. But Jack was gone.

"Jack!" Ben flung the beam of the flashlight out into the darkness of the tunnel. The light revealed his brother several yards away, laboring with all his might against the current.

"Oh, God, help him… Please!" Ben prayed over and over again. Slowly Jack gained ground. Ben reached down a hand to hoist him up. It seemed to take the rest of their strength, but the next moment Jack was on the ledge, both of them heaving and gasping for air, the adrenaline still coursing through their bodies. "What happened?" Ben gasped out.

"My foot slipped as I lifted Jeb. I still can't believe I made it back. I thought I was a goner," Jack answered. They looked at each other, realizing how close they had come.

"I'm glad you made it," Ben whispered, swallowing hard. Jack laid a hand on his brother's shoulder and tried to smile. There was just enough room for them to sit squeezed together. They put Jeb in the middle to keep him warm with Shadow right beside him.

The water continued rising, slowly but steadily. They turned off the flashlight to save the batteries. The fear they felt was tangible. There were no words to express the utter despair that filled them as the darkness pressed in on them and the water relentlessly continued to rise. Even though they were together and alive, hope waned with the realization that they may still drown.

An unknown amount of time passed before Ben flicked on the flashlight. The water was almost level with the ledge. He turned it off. None of them wanted to see their fate rising up before them. After a few moments, he began to pray out loud. His heartrending pleas to the Lord to stop the rising water and rescue them seemed to be drowned out by the ominous silence of the ever-rising water.

"Jack, are we going to die here?" Jeb's voice was small as he huddled between them. "Jack, where is God when we need Him?"

Jack put an arm around his younger brother. Never before had he felt so hopeless. How could he comfort Jeb when he wondered the same things himself? Where was God on this river of despair?

"It's going to be okay," he found himself saying. His words sounded hollow in the vastness of the dark tunnel. Jack swallowed hard and felt the tears choking him. "I love you…both of you, Jeb and Ben." He felt his brothers move closer.

"I love you both, too," Ben said quietly. "I just wish I could see Dad and Mom one last time. I don't think I told them I love them before we left."

Jeb didn't say anything, and Jack realized it was because he was crying, silently, trying his best not to let himself be heard. Jack's eyes filled with tears too.

God, where are You? he silently pleaded. Instantly the Bible verses that they were memorizing in Sunday school came to his mind:

> Whither shall I go from thy spirit?
> Or whither shall I flee from thy presence?
> If I ascend up into heaven, thou art there.
> If I make my bed in hell, behold, thou art there.
> If I take the wings of the morning, and dwell in the uttermost parts of the sea;
> Even there shall thy hand lead me, and thy right hand shall hold me.
> If I say, surely the darkness shall cover me; even the night shall be light about me.
> Yea, the darkness hideth not from thee;
> But the night shineth as the day: the darkness and the light are both alike to thee.

Psalm 139:7-12 (KJV)

Jack began to say them out loud, and Ben and Jeb soon joined him. A word was missed here and there, but they finished it. "The darkness and the light are both alike to thee." Yes, God was with them in this dark place. He saw them, knew their thoughts, and knew the danger of the rising water. He was right next to them. He had helped them this far. He would help them get out of this river of despair alive or welcome them into His heavenly arms.

A few hours later, the storm finally ended. Only after it had reached the boys' waists did the water finally begin to recede. The three wet and cold brothers fell into a peaceful slumber, huddled together on the ledge, wrapped in the knowledge they were not alone. God *was* with them. The panic flowed away, leaving behind a tranquil comfort that was warmer than any campfire.

CHAPTER 9

With rain dripping off the eaves, Sara Talon absentmindedly swept the front porch. Deep in thought, she did not hear Royal bound up the steps two at a time until the last second. She whirled around, letting out a startled cry.

"Are you all right, Sara?"

"Yes, you just startled me." She paused, dropping her eyes. "Royal, I'm very concerned about the boys."

"That's what I was coming to tell you. I feel the same. So I've decided to take Duke and ride up to Lost Cabin and investigate." Royal gave his wife a reassuring hug.

Sarah didn't ask any questions, just nodded.

"Be careful. I'll be praying for you," she replied as she stood up on tiptoes and kissed him good-bye.

By the time Royal reached Lost Cabin, the rain had stopped; the air was cool and the sky overcast and steely gray. There was no evidence that the boys had spent the night there, and Royal's heart sank inside him. The worry became a gnawing fear. *Dear Lord, help me find them. Help them to be okay. Take away this fear, Lord*, he prayed.

He decided to head up hill to where the boys said they had found the helmet and dagger. Less than an hour later, Duke's head and ears came up, and he whinnied. Immediately a horse answered from up above them. A few minutes later, he came upon the boys' mounts huddled together, wet and bedraggled, with their lead lines tangled in brush.

"Jack! Ben! Jeb!" Royal's yells carried across the mountainside, but they went unanswered. He called again with no reply. As he dismounted, he saw an unfamiliar pack leaning against the base of some rocks. It was completely soaked and looked as though it had been there for many days. He squatted to examine the contents of the pack and the entrance to the cave came into view. It was then Royal knew his search was just beginning.

He went back to Duke, hobbled him with the other horses, grabbed his flashlight from his saddle pack, and entered the cave. He yelled for the boys again, his voice echoing back to him from the musty interior. His flashlight fell first on the boys' sleeping bags and saddles. At least he knew the boys had been there. He then saw the skeleton, the belongings of the Spanish soldier, and the sacks of gold.

His mind did not have long to dwell on what he found before his flashlight beam caught the entrance to the tunnel. He entered it and, after several yards, noticed a modern rifle leaning against the wall. With his brow furrowed, Royal quickened his pace.

The beginning of the steep chute was suddenly in front of him. He stopped so he could let his flashlight beam reveal what was in front of him. In doing so, the light caught the vein of gold in the ceiling, and his mouth dropped open as he marveled at the size. He slowly moved forward, shining his flashlight down the steep tunnel below him. It took a bit for his eyes to adjust and his mind to realize there was a pile of debris far down the tunnel. It made his blood run cold.

"Jack! Ben! Jeb!" he yelled again for his boys. Again his voice returned unanswered. He reviewed in his mind what he knew. The boys entered the cave, found the gold vein, were followed by a stranger with a rifle, and then something terrible happened that caused the pile of debris to end up at the bottom of the tunnel.

He wiped a hand across his mouth, sick to his stomach. He wondered what was beyond the debris. Were the boys caught in it? Were they dead? "Oh, Lord, please let them be safe," he pleaded. Or were they alive, trapped underground?

"I'm going to bring help, boys!" he yelled down the tunnel, hoping they would hear and know he was coming. "I'll be back with help soon!" he shouted as he turned and ran back up the tunnel.

Jack stirred, his muscles stiff, his bones aching. It was pitch black. He could feel Ben and Jeb waking up too. The flashlight flickered and came on. Reality came back: the fall down the tunnel, the endless riverbed, the wet and the cold and little food, the flash flood, barely making it to the ledge, the fear that had gripped them. It all came back in a sickening rush. Thankfully the words of Psalm 139 came back also, bringing peace again to their underground prison.

The water beneath them was only a foot and a half deep now and not flowing as swift. Ben flicked on the flashlight. Jeb looked pale, and his eyes revealed the pain he was experiencing. Shadow stood up, shook herself, ready to go when they were.

"Jack…" Ben's voice held fresh despair. "Your knapsack…" To his dismay, Jack saw that most of the contents had been lost in their flight back up the riverbed. It had fallen open when Ben had reached in to get the flashlight.

Jack and Ben immediately took stock of their remaining supplies. They had four sandwiches, two cans of beans, thirty odd matches, six batteries, and five lone candles. That was it. They sat in silence for a moment, contemplating reality.

"Let's each eat a sandwich and split a can of beans," Jack said quietly. "We need our strength more than anything right now." They ate slowly, savoring each bite, giving some to Shadow who looked at them with large, thankful eyes. The food helped to revive them all. Jack prayed asking the Lord to lead them out.

"All right…" Jack looked at his brothers and patted Shadow's head. "Let's get going."

⟫⟩●⟨⟪

Royal pushed Duke as hard as he dared back down the mountain to home. He rushed into the house, leaving muddy prints down the hallway into the kitchen. He picked up the phone.

"Operator? Yes, this is an emergency. I need the Larimer County Sheriff's office," he said.

As with most party lines, as soon as he had picked up the phone, several others in the Valley picked up to listen. Sara came into the kitchen, seeing the muddy footprints, and heard her husband ask for the sheriff's department.

"Sheriff, this is Royal Talon," he began. His voice grew distant as the blood began to rush in Sara's ears. She took a deep breath and started to pray, "Dear Lord, protect my sons." Then she turned and immediately began to fill a knapsack with things she knew her husband would need for the search: a set of clothes, food, a flashlight and batteries, a compass—anything she thought would be useful.

Royal finished with the sheriff by asking him to alert Colorado State University (CSU) to the need for a geologist and an archeologist to handle the artifacts in the cave. He then called the Forest Service and informed the district ranger what had taken place and the need for help to search for his sons. He hung up and made one last phone call over to the dining hall to one of the staff members.

"Start rounding up all the lanterns, rope, and pulleys you can. I need everyone to meet in the dining hall in ten minutes." Royal changed into dry clothes, put his work boots on by the backdoor, and apologized for the muddy prints leading into the kitchen. Sara laid her hand on his arm and looked into his face.

"Just bring our boys home safe, Royal," she said, her voice trembling. Royal nodded and bowed his head and prayed.

"We've got to keep living out our faith, Sara," he said when he had finished. "We can't doubt God now. We have to trust Him, whatever the outcome. We have to remember He's always faithful."

It was her turn to nod, silent tears slipping down her cheeks. Royal kissed his wife and was gone. Thanks to the party line, within half an hour the entire community mobilized as word spread that the Talon boys were trapped underground. Men and boys came to assist with the search and rescue; women came to keep Sara company while she waited.

Four hours later, with Royal leading, the search party had packed, organized, and reached the cave entrance. During the journey, Royal had informed the sheriff and the CSU officials about the skeleton, the bags of gold, and the other artifacts.

"There are two issues," Royal said, guiding Duke around a tree stump in the path. "Number one is to find my boys and get them out safely and number two, the preservation of the skeleton and the artifacts…in that order."

They all agreed. The team from CSU would secure the site to make sure no one walked away with anything in the hubbub of the search. A second group would work on getting through the pile of debris.

The rescue team assembled at the top of the chute near where the first platform once stood. They looked in wonder at the rich vein of gold and then at the steepness of the slide leading to the debris jam. Even as they stood there, small pieces of rock and debris fell, landing far below, the sound ominous. No one missed the gravity of their mission.

The boys had burned through three more candles. They were exhausted. Even though they were encouraged to see the water gradually receding, it was still high enough to make their progress painfully slow. They came to another watercourse, paused, and blew out the candle. This time instead of pitch blackness, there was a dim light coming from around a corner in the main watercourse.

"Hey, look there's light up ahead!" Ben exclaimed. Jack quickly relit the fourth candle, and they hurried forward toward the growing light. Suddenly they splashed into a large, open cavern. Light was streaming down from a hole in the ceiling that was at least fifty feet above them. Jack blew out the candle, and they all stood transfixed—even Shadow—squinting in the bright sunlight. Slowly their eyes adjusted after days of only dim light.

"Look," Ben breathed. Their eyes followed his finger, pointing to a ledge ten feet high on the cavern wall below the hole in the ceiling. There was a skeleton wearing buckskins. "I'll bet that's Grandpa's old friend that disappeared. Remember? He told us about him at his birthday party," Ben said.

"He must have fallen through the skylight," Jack said quietly as they stood in reverent silence. Above the ledge, the wall was smooth granite for twenty feet up before there were even the tiniest cracks. They could see that there was no way to get to the skylight. It was no use. The despair was great—to see the outside and not be able to get out. Would that be their fate? Would they die without anyone finding them until decades later?

"The light is fading," Jeb said, his lips set tight against the pain of his shoulder.

"It must be evening again," Jack said as he turned and found a large rock for Jeb to sit against. "There are some dry areas here. Let's rest for a while then continue on. If we can't find a way out soon, we'll come back here."

CHAPTER 10

There was no doubt in anyone's mind about who was in charge of the rescue operation. Royal Talon was six two, 260 pounds of decisive, focused energy. He was convinced that they were conducting a rescue operation, not a recovery operation. Some of the men had their doubts, but they dared not say anything. They pitied anyone who would lose a child in such a tragic way, let alone all three of their sons at once. They hoped rather than believed that they would find the boys alive.

The rescue team rigged up two lines and lowered Royal and the deputy sheriff down to the top of the debris jam. Once there, the two men worked silently as they attached ropes to the logs jammed in the pile. Once finished, large canvas bags were lowered for them to fill with loose rocks, wood, and other debris. They were hoisted up, dumped outside, and hoisted back down to be used again.

Over the last several hours, Jeb's condition had worsened. He could not walk without support, he was sweating profusely, his eyes could not focus well, and his speech was incoherent. Jack laid the back of his hand against Jeb's forehead. His eyes met Ben's.

"He's burning up," Jack said. He dipped his hand in the stream and bathed Jeb's face with water. Ben fumbled in the knapsack and grabbed out the last sandwich.

"Let's give him this," Ben suggested.

"Only half of it. We'll need to keep up our energy too. It looks like we may have to carry him soon," Jack replied quietly. They fed Jeb, afraid that it might be the last time, and then the two of them finished off the sandwich in one bite each. They pushed on, slowly making their way down the riverbed. After a few minutes, they came to a series of rapids that stretched in front of them.

"Help me get Jeb on my back," Jack said to Ben. "He won't make it walking."

"First I've got to switch out the batteries, Jack. They're fading," Ben said. The darkness engulfed them as Ben emptied out the old batteries and put the new ones in. He flicked it on, but there was no light.

"Turn it on," Jack said impatiently.

"I did."

They stood in silence while Ben opened the flashlight and put two different ones in. They both sighed with relief when the light came on. There was only one set of batteries remaining. The boys were also down to their last candle. Their hope was dwindling along with their supply of light.

Ben walked beside Jack through the rapids in case his brother slipped with Jeb on his back. Shadow took up the rear. Suddenly another watercourse appeared in the riverbed from the right. Ben turned the flashlight off as they stood in the rapids, the water rushing around their legs. There was no light or air movement so they continued on.

A couple hours later the endless, winding, snakelike riverbed ended in a small pool. Ben pointed the flashlight to a small whirlpool near the middle, "The water continues underground from here." The reality that they had reached the end of their journey slowly washed over them. The only thing behind them was the skylight, but the batteries or candles would be used up before they got there. Maybe their fate was to die alone in the dark, where no one would ever find them.

Exhausted, wet, cold, and discouraged almost to despair, they huddled together on a rock and shared the last of their food: a can of beans. After they turned off the flashlight to try to sleep, Jack pleaded quietly, "Dear Lord, please help us."

The rescue team worked nonstop hauling out loose debris, and finally they were ready to dislodge the main jam. From above, several men heaved on the ropes tied to strategic logs and pulled them free. The roar of the debris falling down the chute was deafening. A great cloud of dust shot back up, covering Royal and the deputy as they hung suspended.

Once the dust settled, they repelled down to the bottom, followed quickly by more men, and began the arduous process of sorting through the debris. The unspoken fear among them all was that the boys were in the tangled pile now at the bottom of chute.

Royal worked in silence, trying to prepare himself for finding his sons, knowing that, if they did, it would only be their bodies. He knew their souls were already safe in heaven. Yet all the time he worked, he was filled with a growing peace that Jack and Ben and Jeb were still alive.

After several minutes of hard work, one of the men stopped, stepped to the side, and sat down to rest. His hand felt something, and he looked over so that the beam from his head lantern illuminated it. He squinted. It looked like a piece of brown paper bag. He swiftly moved the rock holding it down, and held it up.

"Hey, look at this!" he yelled as he stood and waved the bag over his head. They soon crowded around him, reading Ben's note saying the boys were alive and were heading downriver.

———⟫●⟪———

"Jeb…Jeb, wake up." Jack vigorously shook his youngest brother. He fumbled for the flashlight as his younger brother thrashed around in his sleep, mumbling incoherently. He flipped it on, looking at Jeb. Ben was rubbing his eyes, trying to focus. "He doesn't look good at all," Jack said. "He's getting worse. His clothes are still wet, and he's burning up all the same."

Jack tore off one of his shirtsleeves, dipped it in the water, and laid it over Jeb's forehead. There was nothing else he could do. He was no doctor, but he sensed his brother's health was in grave danger. Although there was no way of knowing exactly how long they had slept, it really didn't matter. It seemed like they had always been walking the riverbed, trapped underground.

Jack flipped off the flashlight. "We'd better get moving. It's a ways back to the skylight."

"At least there's light there," Ben said.

"I know Dad and Mom are looking for us by now. They *have* to be…" Jack's voice trailed off. Both boys were swallowing back tears of despair and hopelessness. They prepared for the hike back to the skylight, transferring everything into one knapsack for Ben to carry. Then Jack lifted Jeb on his back and turned to leave.

At the last second, he wistfully looked back at the pool. Something caught his eye, and he did a double take. He saw an area in the pool that was emanating a gray light. His heart leapt in his throat. "Turn off the flashlight! Quick!" he shouted. Ben flipped off the flashlight.

"What is it?"

They stood in the darkness, their eyes readjusting. "Look at the pool, at the far end. Do you see anything?" Jack asked. Ben looked.

"The water seems to be glowing," he answered. As their eyes continued to readjust, the area of light became more defined. The whirlpool appeared to be the entrance to an underground tunnel, drawing the water down and away. But how long was it? Where was the water being taken? What was the source of the light?

"We need to pray," Jack said. They bowed their heads and prayed for wisdom. When they were done, they stood quietly, their eyes fixed on the whirlpool. While they were staring, they noticed the light in the whirlpool dim for about thirty seconds and then return to its original intensity. Then after another minute, the light dimmed again and once again brightened after a short time.

"You know what that is? It's the clouds going over the sun," Ben said. "That tunnel is a way to the outside and it must not be too long. It's worth the risk to me. I say let's go! I know we can do it."

"You know I think you're right. Let's put Shadow through first," Jack answered. "We'll wait, and then you can go. I'll wait a little longer, and then I'll come through holding on to Jeb." The far end of the pool glowed. There was no need to stop and think about it any longer; it was simply time to go.

It took all their strength to lift Shadow and throw her into the whirlpool. They felt sick as they watched her desperately try to paddle out of the whirlpool current and then become wide-eyed with panic as the water swiftly pulled her under and into the tunnel. Ben took off his knapsack, hugging it to his chest. He smiled bravely at his brother, and they shook hands. He took a couple of deep breaths, held his nose closed with one hand, and jumped into the whirlpool. Jack watched the whirlpool suck him under and into the tunnel.

Jack and Jeb were now alone. The darkness seemed to press him from behind, urging him to jump. He counted slowly to thirty, feeling numb, trying not to think as he took off Jeb's glasses and put them in his back pocket. "Jeb, take a couple of deep breaths, and when I say jump, jump with all you've got," he told his brother. Jack breathed deeply and locked arms with Jeb.

"Jump!"

CHAPTER 11

The icy chill of the water struck them full force. The whirlpool greedily sucked them into the tunnel. The current was extremely swift, banging them against the sides of the narrow tunnel. Jack desperately clung to Jeb's arm, praying they would make it out alive. They could see the light rushing toward them, but what seemed like a lifetime was in reality only fifteen or twenty seconds. Suddenly they popped to the surface, gasping for air.

The bright sunlight blinded them, giving Jack the brief thought that maybe they were really drowning and that the light was heaven. He struggled, kicking his feet with all his might, holding Jeb with one arm and swimming with the other. The current propelled them downstream, the rushing river larger than normal due to the heavy rainfall. They were out of control, hitting boulders, trying to keep their heads above the water.

Faintly, they heard a familiar sound. It was barking! *Shadow?* Unexpectedly, a hand grabbed Jack's arm and pulled them across the current toward a rock. It was Ben. He was wedged between two rocks to give him stability. They began the fight to the riverbank together. Ben pulled Jack and Jack dragged Jeb.

All this time Shadow barked incessantly from the river bank, as if to cheer them on, urging them to try harder, not to give up. Jeb felt like his shoulder had been ripped from his body, but he tried his best through the fever, the weakness, and pain to help his brothers' struggle toward land.

Finally, they dragged themselves onto the bank and lay there heaving, wet, and utterly exhausted. Jeb cried from the pain and from relief. They had made it out and were safe, even Shadow. She came to lick their faces, wagging her tail, looking none the worse for wear. She had already forgiven them for unceremoniously throwing her into the whirlpool.

The four of them rested on the riverbank, overwhelmed with thankfulness. One by one, they each thanked the Lord for His complete deliverance and His merciful protection.

"I can't believe we almost turned back," Jack said after they prayed. "I still don't know what made me look back at the pool."

Ben looked over at him. "God made you look back," he replied confidently. They all knew without a doubt that this was true. They were different boys now than when they had entered the cave. They were older in ways, wiser, stronger, and closer to the Lord than they had ever been. They had lived a lifetime in just a few short days. They lay in silence for a few minutes, bruised, injured, and weary, basking in the healing warmth of the sun.

"We've got to figure out where we are," Jack said, sitting up and looking around them. "I'm not positive, but I think this is the North St. Vrain River."

"I think you're right. Remember we crossed the North St. Vrain on our bike trip up to Allenspark last summer," Ben agreed. Jack was standing up now, wringing out his shirt.

"If we head upstream, we'll eventually run into Highway 7," Jack said. "Let's get going!"

Jeb mumbled something and Jack stooped down next to him.

"I can't hear you, Jeb."

"I can't see," Jeb distinctly pronounced each word.

"Oh!" Jack felt for his brother's glasses in his back pocket and drew them out. They were a mangled mess.

"You smashed my glasses," Jeb said with a fake pout, a smile tugging at the corner of his mouth.

"Yeah, I guess I was too busy saving your life." Jack smiled, ruffling his brother's wet hair. Ben laughed, and soon all three were laughing.

"I'm glad we all still have our sense of humor, but we need to move on and get home," Jack said. He could tell Jeb's energy would not last after the initial excitement died down, the fever never having broken. And they were all weak from hunger.

He motioned to Ben. "Help me get him up." The thought of a warm, comfortable bed and a home-cooked meal and the fact that they could now see where they were going, spurred them on in spite of the rough terrain. Supporting Jeb between them, they had to stop and rest often, which made their progress frustratingly slow.

When they came to the edge of Cabin Creek flowing in from the north, it was twice its normal size due to the deluge of the rainstorm.

"How are we ever going to get across that?" Ben wondered out loud. After assessing the possibilities, Jack pointed upstream at an uprooted tree lying out in the stream lodged between some boulders.

"Look, we can climb out to the end of that log and only have to jump the remaining six feet to the bank," Jack offered.

"I agree. How about if I go first, followed by Jeb? We both can steady him until the gap, and then he will have to jump the gap by himself," answered Ben as he turned to head upstream, Shadow ahead of him.

"Do you think you can jump that far, Jeb?" Jack asked.

Jeb was trying to readjust the sling around his arm when Jack asked him the question. Jeb squinted to try and focus on the jump he would have to make, but without his glasses, his imagination had to suffice.

"I've jumped farther," Jeb replied confidently, shrugging his shoulders. "Besides, we don't have much of an option, do we?" Before they could say anything else, Shadow leaped onto the tree, trotted to the edge, and jumped with ease onto the opposite bank. She looked back as if to say, "Hurry up! See how easy it is?"

The boys slowly climbed out onto the tree using its branches for support, the creek raging underneath them. Jeb slipped once with the boys steadying him. Ben reached the end of the tree, steadied his feet, and lunged for the river's edge. He landed just on the top edge of the steep bank and fell forward on the ground. Ben quickly stood up and grabbed a large stick and called out to Jeb, "Okay, you can do it. Give it all you've got! I've got a stick here for you to grab on to if you need it!"

Jeb securely planted his feet, squinted his eyes to focus on the bank, and pushed off from the log. He stretched out his left arm as far as possible to try to reach the stick. His fingers closed around the end of the stick, but his feet plunged into the icy creek. His weak hold on the stick could not prevent him from being swept away downstream.

Ben's face reflected the horror and helplessness as he watched his brother disappear. Jack immediately jumped in after his brother and caught up with him in a few seconds, wrapping him in a bear hug. They now found themselves back in the middle of the St. Vrain River being pulled along by the current, bobbing like corks heading downstream. Jeb was desperately trying to keep his head above the rapids, and Jack was trying to steer them away from large rocks with his feet. Suddenly, they came to a jarring halt.

"Aah!" Jeb screamed in pain when his injured shoulder hit squarely on the rock.

"Hang on, Jeb," Jack yelled. "We'll be out of this soon." They were wedged between two rocks with the water flowing around and over them. Jack pushed up on the rocks and scanned the area around them. He could see there were a lot more visible boulders in this wider area of the river. He used this to their advantage as they made their way across the stream to the bank. He boosted Jeb up on his shoulders then up onto the top of the riverbank. Jack was right behind him and flopped down beside Jeb, breathing hard and thanking the Lord once again for saving their lives.

Ben saw a grouping of huge boulders that would be a great lookout to see what was happening downstream. "Come on, Shadow! Follow me!" Ben scrambled to the top of the highest boulder and scanned downstream.

What he saw filled him with relief. He could see Jack and Jeb sprawled on the riverbank.

"Are you two all right?" Ben shouted through cupped hands in the direction of his brothers downstream. All Jack could do was raise a hand in reply. As they rested, Jack realized that they were on the opposite side of the river from Ben and had traveled fifty yards in just a few minutes.

Jack got up and told his brother, "Sorry, Jeb, no time to rest. We've got to start walking." Jack gave Jeb a hand up. "Here, put your left hand in my rear pocket of my jeans and follow my lead." They once again started upstream and were soon abreast of Ben on the opposite side.

"I thought you two were goners," yelled Ben. Jack just waved and smiled.

After two hours of walking parallel to each other on opposite sides of the river, a bridge rose up in front of them that crossed over the St. Vrain River. They quickened their step as they saw the end of their journey and heard a car approaching in the distance.

Jack carried Jeb on his back the last few hundred yards to the edge of the highway. When they popped over the top, Ben and Shadow ran over. Ben reached out to help Jack gently lay Jeb down near the road, and they both sat down next to him exhausted. A few seconds later, a beat-up Jeep flew around the bend and passed them, showering them with pebbles.

"Mr. Hondo," Jack shouted as he jumped to his feet. The older man slammed on his brakes, backed up, and jumped out of the vehicle.

"You three are supposed to be lost," he said with a wry smile. Jack suddenly felt released from the heavy weight of responsibility. He had gotten his brothers out, by God's grace. Now Mr. Hondo was here to take over.

"Can you take us home?" Jack managed to say.

⸺⬦⬦⸺

The six miles to home flew by. As they pulled up in front of their house, Jack and Ben jumped out of the front seat. Sara was looking out the window and ran out to meet them, showering them with kisses as she gathered them close. Tears of joy coursed down her cheeks.

"Where's Jeb?" her voice trembled.

"He's in the back seat, Mom, lying down," Jack reassured her. Sara went to her youngest son. More tears stung her eyes when she saw him.

"He's got a broken collarbone and a pretty bad fever," Jack said. Mr. Hondo picked up Jeb and carried him into the house. Everyone waiting with Sara now gathered around them, rejoicing. They radioed the command post set up outside the cave with the good news.

Six hours later, the good news was brought by two workers as Royal's team reached the cavern with the skylight. "Your boys are something else, Royal," the deputy told him. "This is the roughest rescue mission I've ever been on, and I'm a grown man. I can't imagine just how hard it was for them. I'm so glad they are safe."

Royal smiled and led them all in a prayer of thanksgiving. As they headed back, the workers who came with the news filled them in on what had happened in their absence.

"We found a body in the rubble at the bottom of the chute," one of them said.

"Can you tell who it is?" Royal asked.

"Yes, it's John Holt," replied one of them.

Nothing more was said. Royal pushed everything else out of his mind but the thought of getting home, seeing his boys, and reassuring himself that they were safe.

<hr />

"Sara! Boys!" Royal flew into the house, forgetting about his boots and tracking mud down the hall. Sara came out of the boy's room. Her husband's eyes asked the question he could not bring himself to voice.

"They're all okay," she said. "Doc Mills just got here, and he's looking at Jeb right now. He has a broken collarbone and a fever. Jack and Ben are just exhausted and have a lot of bruises and cuts."

They stopped in the doorway. The three boys had bathed and already eaten their first hot meal. Jack and Ben sat on the end of Jeb's bed watching the doctor.

"Dad!" Jeb's voice was weak, but his smile was big. Jack and Ben looked around.

"Dad!" Ben exclaimed.

"Hey, Dad, we're home!" Jack shouted. Both of them ran to him, and he gathered them in a big hug. He walked over to the bed and rested a hand on his youngest son's head.

"I'm so glad you're home safe, Son," he smiled, squatting down beside the bed so he was level with Jeb.

"You were coming for us, weren't you, Dad?" Jeb asked confidently.

"Yes, I was coming for you, son. You bet," Royal replied, and then he asked Doc Mills, "What do you think, Doc?"

"He's got a fractured collarbone and fever that doesn't seem to be giving up. I'd like to take him into Estes where I can watch him and sling that shoulder properly." He met Royal's eyes. "From some of the things your boys have been telling me, they're all very lucky to be alive."

"Oh, it wasn't luck, sir," Jack interjected. "It was God." And looking in his dad's eyes, he said, "Dad, we lied to you and Mom about the gold and the cave. It was wrong, and I'm awfully sorry."

"Apology accepted, son. But let's not worry about that now. You and your brothers will work that all out later," he said, smiling with a wink.

———————

At 5:00 a.m. on the second Saturday after the boys got home, Royal walked into the boys' room and turned on the lights. "All right, boys, get up. Breakfast is waiting! Hurry up. You have work to do!"

Jeb groggily put on his new glasses and asked, "What about me? I'm injured!"

His dad smiled and replied, "You'll work with me until you're healed up. Now let's get moving!" It took no further urging from their dad; they knew he meant business, so they quickly dressed and headed downstairs.

Near the end of their breakfast of eggs, toast, hash browns, bacon, and orange juice, Royal Talon cleared his throat and began, "Boys, Proverbs 22:1 says, 'A man's good name is more important than great riches.' When you decided to lie about the gold and cave, you damaged your good name, and that is something that is very hard to earn back. I know you have asked Mom and me for forgiveness, but you also hurt your relationship with the Lord. If you haven't already, you need to confess that to Him and ask His forgiveness as well." Their food forgotten, Royal had his boys' full attention.

"I know for a fact that good, old hard work gives a man time to think and ponder his actions. So every Saturday, starting today until the Spanish soldier's remains are put to rest, you will work from sunrise to sunset on chores that I will assign you. This is above and beyond your normal chores that you do after school." His face softened as he went on. "Proverbs also says, 'Rebuke a wise man and he will love you. Give instruction to a wise man and he will be yet wiser.' Now here are today's lists. Finish your breakfast, and let's get to work!"

Twenty-four Saturdays later, on a cold and clear winter day, the boys and a group of men held a small ceremony near the now gated entrance to the cave. Sergeant Jimenez was formally laid to rest; a Catholic priest from St. Malo conducted the service. The archeological team from CSU had long ago finished cataloging and preserving the cave. It was a historical site now.

Geologists had a field day exploring and mapping the underground watercourses throughout Tahosa Valley, previously unknown to anyone. They discovered that the courses had formed as water sought the least line of resistance and moved through fissures in the granite underneath the Valley. Over time, erosion and frost expansion created small underground cracks that develop into full-blown underground rivers.

And the gold? The boys each got one big nugget, and the federal government got the rest. Royal and Sara claimed the nugget that the boys had originally taken out of the cave.

Those days on the river of despair taught Jack, Ben, and Jeb what it really meant to live out their faith and rely solely on their heavenly Father. Through the danger and hardship, an unbreakable bond had been forged between the three brothers.

As the group snowshoed back down the mountain, the boys, glad to finally be done with their extra chores, began thinking of the possibility of new adventures. Ben decided to stir up a little adventure right there and molded a hard-packed snowball.

"Hey, Jeb!" he mischievously called. Jeb stopped and turned to look at Ben and was hit full in the face with the snowball, sending his glasses flying and shattering them on a boulder nearby.

Coming soon, another Talon Family Story:
Winter Chase!